Ladybird books are widely available, but in case of
difficulty may be ordered by post or telephone from:

Ladybird Books – Cash Sales Department
Littlegate Road  Paignton  Devon TQ3 3BE
Telephone 0803 554761

A catalogue record for this book is available
from the British Library

Published by Ladybird Books Ltd  Loughborough  Leicestershire  UK

Printed in EC

# THE TALE OF
# SAMUEL
# WHISKERS ™

Based on the original and authorized story
by Beatrix Potter
Ladybird Books in association with Frederick Warne

Once upon a time there was an old cat, called Mrs Tabitha Twitchit, who was an anxious parent. She had three kittens, Tom and his sisters, Moppet and Mittens. Mrs Tabitha Twitchit used to lose her kittens continually, and whenever they were lost they were always in mischief!

One baking day Mrs Tabitha Twitchit
decided to shut them in a cupboard.
"And there you'll stay, my two young
rascals, until my baking is finished,"
she said, catching Moppet and Mittens.
But she could not find Tom anywhere.

Tom Kitten did not want to be shut in
a cupboard. He looked about for a
good place to hide, and decided
upon the chimney. The fire had only
just been lit, so it was not hot.

Tom Kitten jumped right up into the fireplace and landed on a ledge inside the chimney. "I cannot go back," Tom Kitten said, looking down. "If I slip I might fall into the fire and singe my beautiful tail and my little blue jacket."

He decided to climb right to the top of the chimney, and to get out on the roof, and try to catch sparrows.

Meanwhile, Mrs Tabitha Twitchit was still searching for Tom, so Moppet and Mittens pushed open the cupboard door and came out. They went straight to the dough which had been left to rise in a pan in front of the fire.

"Shall we make dear little muffins?" said Mittens to Moppet.

"Oh, do let's," replied Moppet excitedly.

Just at that moment somebody knocked at the front door. Moppet jumped into a flour barrel in a fright. Mittens ran away to the dairy and hid in an empty pot on a stone shelf where the milk pans stood.

Mrs Tabitha Twitchit came tearfully downstairs. "Come in, Cousin Ribby, come in. I've lost my dear son Thomas. I'm afraid the rats have got him," she sobbed. "Oh, dear me – now Moppet and Mittens are gone, too!" she cried. "They have both got out of the cupboard."

"Your Tom's a bad kitten, Cousin Tabitha," said Cousin Ribby. "But I'm not afraid of rats. I will help you to find him. Now, just where would a naughty little kitten hide?"

Cousin Ribby and Mrs Tabitha
Twitchit set to work to search the
house thoroughly. They poked under
the beds with Cousin Ribby's
umbrella, and they rummaged in
cupboards. They even fetched a
candle and looked inside a clothes
chest in one of the attics. They could
not find Tom, Moppet or Mittens
anywhere.

Meanwhile, Tom
Kitten was getting
very frightened!
He climbed up,
and up, and up
the chimney,
through inches of
soot. It was very
confusing in the dark,
and Tom Kitten felt quite lost.

All at once he fell head over heels
down a hole and landed on a heap of
very dirty rags.

Opposite to Tom – as far away
as he could sit – was an
enormous rat.

"What do you mean by tumbling into my bed all covered with soot?" said the old man rat, chattering his teeth.

"Anna Maria! Anna Maria!" squeaked the rat, whose name was Samuel Whiskers. There was a pattering noise and an old woman rat poked her head round a rafter.

"What have we here?" cried Anna
Maria gleefully. "A tasty morsel
indeed!" She ran towards Tom Kitten,
and before he knew what was
happening, his coat had been pulled
off and he was rolled in a bundle and
tied with string in very tight knots.

"Anna Maria," said Samuel Whiskers, "make me a kitten dumpling roly-poly pudding for my dinner."

"Hmmm, it requires dough, and a pat of butter and a rolling pin," said Anna Maria.

So the two rats set off, leaving Tom Kitten wriggling about under the floor of the attic and mewing for help. He could not make anybody hear him, except a spider, which did not offer to help.

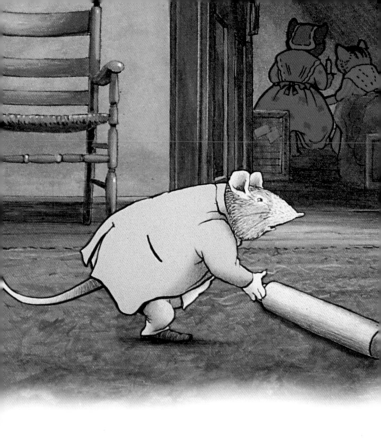

Samuel Whiskers went boldly down
the front staircase to the dairy to get
the butter. He made a second journey
for the rolling pin, which he pushed
in front of him with his paws.

Anna Maria went down to the kitchen by way of the skirting board to steal the dough. She borrowed a small saucer, and scooped up the dough with her paws.

"He is rather a *large* kitten for his age," she muttered to herself, scooping up another pawful.

Presently the rats came back and started to turn Tom Kitten into a dumpling. First they smeared him with butter and then rolled him in the dough.

"Will not the string be indigestible, Anna Maria?" asked Samuel Whiskers. Anna Maria said she thought it was of no consequence.

Tom Kitten bit and spat, and mewed and wriggled. And the rolling pin went roly-poly, roly, roly, poly, roly.

Above the rats in the attic, Cousin Ribby and Mrs Tabitha Twitchit searched and searched. They both heard the curious roly-poly noise under the attic floor. But there was nothing to be seen, so they returned to the kitchen.

"Here's one of your kittens," said Cousin Ribby, dragging Moppet out of the flour barrel. She seemed very frightened.

"Oh! Mother, Mother," cried Moppet, "there's been an old woman rat in the kitchen, and she's stolen some dough!"

Cousin Ribby and Mrs Tabitha Twitchit took Moppet with them while they went on with their search. In the dairy they found Mittens hiding in an empty pot. "Oh! Mother, Mother," cried Mittens, "there's been an old man rat in the dairy, and he's stolen a pat of butter and the rolling pin!"

"Did we not hear a roly-poly noise in the attic," said Cousin Ribby, "when we were looking in that chest?" Cousin Ribby and Mrs Tabitha Twitchit rushed upstairs. Sure enough the roly-poly noise was still going on under the attic floor.

"Oh my goodness," said Cousin Ribby. "We must send for John Joiner at once."

As soon as John Joiner arrived, pushing a wheelbarrow, Mrs Tabitha Twitchit and Cousin Ribby hurried him into the attic and set him to work.

Beneath the attic floor, Samuel Whiskers and Anna Maria were arguing over the roly-poly pudding.

"His tail is sticking out! You did not fetch enough dough, Anna Maria. And I do not think," said Samuel Whiskers, pausing to take a look at Tom Kitten, "I do *not* think it will be a good pudding. It smells *sooty*."

Anna Maria was about to argue when all at once there began to be other sounds up above – the rasping noise of a saw, and the noise of a dog, scratching and yelping!

"We are discovered and interrupted, Anna Maria," said Samuel Whiskers. "Let us collect our property – and other people's – and depart at once. I fear that we shall have to leave this pudding," he sighed.

So, by the time John Joiner had got some of the attic floor up, there was nothing to be seen except a rolling pin and Tom Kitten in a very dirty dumpling!

Samuel Whiskers and Anna Maria had found a wheelbarrow, belonging to Miss Potter, and were hastily running away down the lane.

Samuel Whiskers and Anna Maria made their way to Farmer Potatoes' barn and hauled their parcels, with a bit of string, to the top of the hay mow.

"Have you, er, given any thought to, er, supper?" Samuel Whiskers asked his wife.

The cat family quickly recovered. The dumpling was peeled off Tom Kitten, and made into a bag pudding, with currants in it to hide the soot. They had to put Tom Kitten into a hot bath to get the butter off!

John Joiner smelt the pudding, but regretted that he had not time to stay to dinner, because he had to deliver a new wheelbarrow to Miss Potter.

After that, there were no more rats for a long time at Mrs Tabitha Twitchit's!